BETWEEN THE TWO LINES

Rajesh Joshi

Translated by
Ratan Chauhan

Pharos Books

ISBN: 978-93-55460-20-2
eISBN: 978-93-55460-21-9

©Author

Publisher: Pharos Books (P) Ltd.
Plot No.-55, Main Mother Dairy Road
Pandav Nagar, East Delhi-110092
Phone: 011-40395855, +14049995474
WhatsApp: +91 8368220032
E-mail: sales@pharosbooks.in
Website: www.pharosbooks.in
First Edition: 2022

Between the Two Lines
Rajesh Joshi

For
Malay ji
Naresh Saxena
and
Vijay Kumar

Contents

Between the two lines

Between the two lines of a poem I am the space
that always looks rather desolate.

It's here that the invisible shadow of a poet often haunts.
I am a hidden galaxy of a poet's cosmos.
Words often avoid trafficking here.
Some Helping Verb or a word left out in a great hurry
sometimes comes and rather sits, ill at ease on some edge,
nasal sounds and some accents keep peering through my
peripheries.

A great many sounds keep dropping here screening
through the words.
Sometimes some such connotations of words stray in that
like the wayward children ran away long back from their
homes.

I am not that passionless or non-vibrant a space that I
look to be,
a pause I am that comes abruptly in between
conversation, wherein there keep drifting the left-overs of
the talks. A number of secret alleys shoot forth from my
alleys that can lead to an unexplored world of the poet
kept hidden from every body.

In this woodland of the illimitable, there keep sporting
multitudinous images rather mysterious.

In the midst of the lofty fencing of words, I am an open
sky wherein the eagles of a poet's dreams have a long
flight. Behind the wall of the unseen, there hid here some
such tunnels
that, through their secret ways
lead to the story of the origin of words.

Before showing yourself in, mind you, you put off your
shoes outside
that there's no sound of your footfalls,
Even an infinitesimal sound from without, will destroy
my entire magical telesma.

25.08.99

Incomplete poems

Incomplete poems keep gazing wistfully after their last
line, at the space left blank on paper.

Incomplete poems cherish a hope that sometime or the
other they will be completed,
somewhere or the other, in some poem their lines will be
made use of.

For days together, they keep knocking at our doors
intermittently, as if reminding us that "we are very much
here about".
It's because of jealousy perhaps that a number of times
they stop gushing forth the new poems.

Some new line is just to gush forth
that pushing it aside quickly, springs forth some
incomplete poem in oblivion.

They are the cows lost in a pasture that tracking down
their way one day come back and lie outside the closed doors
They are the restless souls wandering round us.

But such is not always the case.
Sometimes they keep lying in deep quiet in a corner of
some piece of paper
for days or months together and some times for whole of
life.
Slipping in our lost memories, they hide themselves
somewhere.

More than often we have to call them a number of times
and even then they don't turn up,
a sense of their incompleteness or a certain pride
of being incomplete
turn them so stubborn
that they won't budge from their place.

They do not say anything but it seems that they say,
'Incomplete we are. Well, we are all right that way,
which poem is there that stepped down on the
earth in completeness.

Some how or the other, deleting or adding some most of
the poems are completed or rather completed.

By the way the largest number in the world is that of
the incomplete poems.'

Even in the complete poems somewhere or the other
there
remains a certain incompleteness.
To every perfect poem, another poet
wants to write in a different way
and the beauty is that by doing this
neither the former nor the latter is satisfied.
It always feels to every poet that something is missing
in the poem
that ought to have been, that could be.

20.04.98

Etc.

A few people who owned some position were named,
the rest were Etc.
Etc. were always more in numbers
Etc. would bargain while purchasing vegetables
and after having taken their meals
would go to listen to the speech of certain important
people.
Etc. would increase the number of presence in every
seminar.
Etc. would participate in the rallies, would hold the
banners
and monger slogans.
Etc. would stand in long queues for voting.
They were always given the impression that they are
the ones
who make the Government in this democracy
Etc. would always participate in the agitation
sometimes resulting in their death in police firings.
When they were killed in such police firings
then their names were also told to us
those which were used during their school admission
or those by which some of them would get paid.
Some would still remain Etc. in such accidents also.
The Etc. were afraid of hazards
but when at times they were not frightened
then all others would fear them.

Etc. were the ones who would do all those works
which would make the country and the world move.
However, it would appear to them
as if they are doing so to run their own families.
Etc. were involved everywhere
but their names were mentioned nowhere.
Etc. would often appear only
in the poetry of certain cynical poets.

(Translated from Hindi by Nirupa Joshi)

Helping Verb

Our language has some such make-up
that it won't rather function without a Helping Verb.

In our grammar there are seven kinds of it, seven
days-like
that without asserting themselves keep completing
the incomplete work of a verb.
There in a sentence so smoothly makes its room.
No major change is possible in its position.
Even then, it often puts up with a little pushing it, on or
back.
Sometimes when it is inverted
it changes the whole sentence into a question
Helping Verb signifying a sense of time often takes its
position, at the end of the row of words as if it were a
humble guest, who sat curling himself at the last corner
of a dinner-line.
As for letters and accents it's a very small unit
It has a very small voice
but is the most audible of all.
For a certain period of time, in music, it was considered
a great obstacle.
There in our language was such a time
That the giants writing songs and lyrics,
Wanted to kick it out from the language.
The sharp tricksters of the language left no stone
unturned to keep it out from the language.

but in the widespread prose of life, its presence continued
to be.
Whenever there's a move to keep it out,
language starts looking somewhat scared and rather
anaemic.
Its presence creates a strange stateliness in the entire
phrase
Sometimes, there implied in it a suggestion of a speaker's
intents.

While issuing orders rulers oft make use of a Helping
Verb giving an inkling in their mind.
Its appearance there in the sentence leaves little room for
doubt.

It's as stubborn also as it looks quieter
If it wills, it alone by itself can ruffle the whole sentence.

27.08.99

Our language

Before being called in a language that was simply a bird
and its our language that called it a bird.
Language itself gave that tree a name
while tree was simply a tree beyond our language
and its our language that called it a tree.
Similarly those innumerable rivers, torrents and
mountains,
probably none knew
that what names our language pronounced them.

They had nothing to do with our language.
Language was our convenience.
We were in a damned hurry to change everything in
language.
A stubbornness as to call everything in language as
quickly as we could,
would throw us a little away from those things.
Many a time things whose names we knew,
we knew not their shapes.
We thought that language was a door to know everything
It's on this ground that sometimes some languages
came to hold their sway.
The language of the weak was considered weak and
it would lose the battle.
Languages had their own egos.
It's not known whether trees, stones, birds, rivers, torrents,
winds and animals had their respective languages or not,

but we would continuously try to read a language in them.
So such a turn of mind would shape their language.
We had the impression that its our assumption only that's
the language of the universe.
We had the presumption that through this language
We would read out the whole cosmos.

25.04.98

Missing things

There were stored things missing for years
and a ghost kept watch on them.

Things so common were there that had been forgotten
long before.

There was that whistle with a shape of a sparrow
that would blow 'bul - bul'[1] like when half-filled with
water
When at college, I blew it hiding myself in the grove of
trees,
the girls passing round would look here and there
in a great amazement.

In a childhood photograph, the tricycle that I rode on
was there dust-laden.
One of its wheels was out and was discoloured in many
places,
stubs of pencils badly scribbled were there
that would refuse anymore sharpening,
The drawing-books of boyhood days were there,
in each, picture of which
trees were green and there was the rising sun.
Then perhaps we didn't think that in our world
there ever would reign this much of darkness.

---

1. Nightingale

Toys that had been lost long before were there,
there were kites, their reels were there wound with thread
well-wrought,
there were some old clocks that were said to be stolen
away
Therein that time had stood still till yet.
There were a great many photos and their negatives of
times lost and people missing.

Time gone by still stood there,
some dust had settled on it and it had grown a
little pale

Of those countless things missing a ghost kept watch on.
That ghost too himself was a missing character
that had long before vanished away somewhere from our
childhood stories

That ghost said to me one day that he wanted to go out
from that fort,
but unfortunately he had lost the key of the door of the
fort somewhere.

06.04.98

A wonder of the last days of the twentieth century

In the last days of the twentieth century, an old man
well above eighty
and who had no immovable property
visited a metropolis
where dwelt some of his relations and a friend.

Even before, he would keep visiting this metropolis,
then he would stay with his elder brother only
but three years back the brother passed away.
After his brother's demise it was his first visit
and was rather hesitant.

He went to his nephew and stayed in the same house
that he frequented in his brother's lifetime.
The nephew and his wife showed the same warmth
as they did in former times.

Hardly had passed three or four days that he had a
phone-call
from his niece who was here in this city only.
'It's three days that you are at your nephew's. When
you are calling on us? And listen, not simply a visit,
the days that you stayed at nephew's, you have to stay at
least with us in our house'.

Then one day, suddenly got a phone from his cousin,
'Would you throughout life take me to be a step brother.

When brother was alive, I was helpless. But even now, you
are staying at brother's only...
If you, don't turn up immediately I will definitely kidnap
you.'

Then one day a phone from his friend and he
cursed the old man wholeheartedly.

It was all in the last days of the twentieth century and
that too in a metropolis
The old man was getting moved to tears deep inside,
would mumble himself ... 'everything hasn't been ruined'.
Sitting by himself, somewhere, he wanted to cry out.
He was recalling his boyhood days and the village of
those days.

04.12.98

Wait, children!

Wait, just wait, children
before you cross the road

Let these speedy cars pass on

One that passed in the white car with a swish
that officer isn't in hurry to reach anywhere.
He shows himself in his department around
twelve and sometimes even after.
Days, months, and sometimes years take
that the urgent file on his table moves.

Wait, children!

Let that magistrate's car pass by.
Who would dare to ask him that 'you' rushing in
such a fast car,
how many cases are there pending in your court, for
how many years

They say 'Justice delayed is justice denied'.
But such fine sentences are meant to be spoken
at seminars or are pretty good things for slogans.
A number of times, hearing after hearing, round after
round, a man reaches the court above
and the case here in his court still lies undecided.

Wait, children, wait!,
before crossing the road.

Better, talk not at all of that police officer.
Whether on foot or in a car
as to move speedily is a part of his training.
That's a different question that he is the last to reach
where a happening takes place.

Wait, children, wait!

Just behind this car blowing the siren,
with a tempestuous speed might be coming
some minister's car.
No, no, he isn't in hurry at all to reach anywhere.
He takes, you know, a number of minutes to get up
from his chair with his pot-belly
It's caught in a certain fear that it's so swift.
Safety looks for a blind speed.

Wait, children!
Let them pass by.

Hurriedly, they are to go
for they haven't to reach anywhere.

23.11.98

A few ill-ordered lines about poison

In a number of drugs and the new and the old practices
of treatment, poison is used.

One conspicuous advantage of this piece of knowledge
is that one can get rid of that sensationalism
that's associated with the word poison and viewing
this piece of knowledge a consensus can be
reached in favour of poison,
something very much like the way as it's spoken about
the new economic policy
that a general opinion votes for it

Well, let's come back to the point and
think about a little on poison
and better we escape any digression.
For some time let's put off mentioning the dangers of
poison,
and those people too, that make use of it
getting bored of life and bid adieu to the world.
Just now, we can avoid talking about that poison
also, that everybody knows is being adulterated
in our air, water and bread.

Here I won't make any statement about that poison
also that's killing our freedom by inches.
Slow poison can well be detected in a great many things
Factually, it may be wrong but they go so far to say
that it's there even in the talks of a few people.

Ruling powers have a pretty well knowledge of this poison
and are adept at making use of it.
The inherent nature of slow poison is that
it corrodes life very-very slowly.
In the light of this argument
can one call time a slow poison.

In poison there's something of a strange fascination
charged with fear and a sensation.
There are some poisons, the moment you put them at the
tip of your tongue they kill you.
Some move smoothly and surreptitiously.
Such poisons often are quite alluring and delicious |
Sometimes they get into the habit of man and become
indispensable one day.

As for the taste of poison people's opinions and
experiences largely vary,
for the kinds of poison too, are so widely different.
Hence it's natural
Some poisons are sweet to taste, some quite bitter, so far
that it's also a practice in our language to call
poison that is bitter.
Some poisons work up like a sensation and rush in the body.

The fury of violence can outmatch a thousand time
a snake and a scorpion.
Anyway, whether slow or quick, poison works |
definitely one day or the other.

In the end, I would like to add one more sentence
to these ill-ordered sentences,
poison isn't administered at all like poison
when it's administered to a society
on a broad scale.

04.02.95

On which they count

Stretch out their small hands,
repeatedly beg, showing their stomach say, they are
hungry for days together.
As to move you to the depths, they use almost every tactic.

We have got so used to all these scenes
that often an annoyance is aroused only,
sometimes a flimsy sentimentality too.
The moment we turn our back,
at their own masquerading, burst out laughing,
the children at begging.

Pass remarks on whom
who has turned away without giving alms,
ape one who fumbled out a coin in his pocket.
Both our unkindness and kindness serve subjects
for their masquerading.

In what a horrible apathy we have thrown them.
How bitter is their feel for our society
in which they also have a niche, around its own border-line.

Sometimes they dream a dream too
that the coloured crime-films of our times
have created in their minds
on which they count that, that way, one day
their life also will go a sea-change.

02.07.95

Some lines about the moon

You are a matchless damned cunning thing, Mr Moon,
For how long will you keep playing with people
this chess with no board.

Does it behove you, Sir
this daily masquerading of yours?
Sometimes in the vast orchestral pit of the sky,
you look hung simply like a trumpet.

You, that keep shuffling all the night long,
don't the policemen on patrol interrogate you.
It looks, yours is a damned tight grip over that Dept.
But here's a piece of advice for you and *in gratis*,
smooth and sleek lads like you
shouldn't wander this way night in, night out.
Sir, the habits of this town aren't that good.

One thing, the pleasure of drinking the wine when you
are mirrored in it, is quite apart.
You might be remembering that heroine
that eyeing out your image in her chalice.
Would tease you
that "Don't get a fright, there's no Rahu[2] in the liquor}
and as for 'Rohini[3], she dwells in the skies."

---

2. a demon
3. a constellation

Sometimes when your orb is in full resplendence
there brew up a number of troubles.
Of course, it's rather unwelcome to the petty burglars
your shining up this way.
But they say that professional criminals
become far more active that day,
there grows the palpitation of the people
and the sea starts rising in a great turbulence
throwing shells and oysters on the shores.

They say that you sprang off from the sea itself.
Aren't you, then, Sir, a runaway child, wayward?
That's why at your very sight
the sea springs up so high.

But sometimes, when some patch of cloud, drifting from
somewhere throws a veil over your face,
its tide ebbs away quickly.
There in the dark is audible only
the sound of its footprints dragging on the sands.

Sometimes you are once in a blue moon.
Sometimes imprisoned in the golden halo of narcissism
you look rather very lonely and one, self-indulgent.

It's with your moonbeams that millions of lovers
have quilled billet doux
and poets have penned poems numberless.
God knows, what's there in your person
that to all the loafers, lunatics, madmen and poets,
you look so, so very close to the heart.

03.11.98

The sound of water

That was the magic of water itself
that even the sound of water looked transparent and liquid.

In the sounds drifting towards the sea,
there mingled the sounds of its stepping down
from the mountain,
in its fall there mingled the sound of its springing up.
Of its multitudinous sounds, one was that of its
driping from the roof.
When some pot was put beneath the drip-drop,
then was added to it one more sound of a chime.

Where water dripped,
there would blossom a flower of water.
In the sound of water, there mingled countless sounds
Mother's voice was heard in it time and again.
That voice would often call us inside the home.
One was that of the friends.
There was one more voice that came from within,
that would take us out.

With the sound of water there were associated memories
numberless.
The memory of the pakoras[4] would swim on the tongue
in taste.

4.. fried edible

The paper-boats of our boyhood days
have floated far away.
God knows in what niches and corners
we had forgotten our umbrellas.
There still would tickle us some tales of getting soaked to
the bone.
At night when our eyes were laden with sleep, somewhere
from far the sound of water would call us.
Then slowly would mingle in our dreams
the sound of water.

07.07.99

In this part of the earth

In this part of the earth right this moment,
the shrillest sounds are of the birds chirping.
In this part of the earth right this moment
the most resonant sounds are of the waves dashing
against the shore.

Right this moment, in this part, the sea
is sharpening its wave like a razor on the rock
of the shore.
Is he preparing to shave off the beard of the sky?
Quite close, there are the gentle small sounds
of the dippings,
there the fishes are at frisk.

Right this moment in this part of the earth
the most sonorous sounds are of the trees rustling.

Here the sun is sinking slowly.
Slowly and slowly the moon is rising higher,
quietly, calmly.
In the reminiscences of the nocturnal awakening,
there are countless phases of the moon
but of all, this one is quite apart.

This part of the earth but is merely a part and not more
of our earth.
Alas!

04.04.98

A short sleep and dreams

As showing signs of advancing age,
sleep is getting brief.

Standing on the threshold, some dream is just to step in
that sleep is broken half-way at midnight.

The dream that set out to visit
my sleep only,
might be wandering at this hour, nobody knows
where and on what roads.
It might be, in this chill night of winter, it knocked
the door of someone else's sleep, saying
it's that I set out to step in Rajesh Joshi's
sleep but what to do, his sleep broke half way at mid-night.
It happens so with advancing age
but I am at a loss to understand where should I
spend the night.
If isn't there any dream, in your sleep,
be kind enough to allow me to have a way in your sleep.

It might be it's rather hesitant as to enter
someone else's sleep.

As for happening, anything may happen. There are
innumerable possibilities.

It might be, it hasn't visited anyone,
might be, it has turned back that it will visit
some other night.

It's probable that in this mishap of advancing age,
a dream might have perished perhaps.

15.01.99

The dwarf

Once again this doubt assailed me
that my size wouldn't grow anymore.

He came running swiftly
and crossed over me.
I was just to stop him
but he didn't allow me anytime at all.
The voice was just on the brink of my lip
that he crossed and skipped over
well ahead

'Getting up, trying to get up', in this mood,
my laziness was lying
reclining its head on the pillow.

He wasn't very very sharp,
he was just like me
say my facsimile.
He just had a chance
and without losing he, encashed it.
Perhaps, he had been in a lurk,
might be, it suddenly struck him
but he crossed over.

And once again this doubt assailed me
that my size wouldn't grow anymore.

18.07.74

The man walking in sleep

The somnambulist doesn't know that he is in
the habit of walking in his sleep

The somnambulist gets up in the dead of night,
turns on all the lights of the entire house,
opening the door outside
comes out on a lonely road.
He walks on the road that's really a road
as if he is walking on some road of a dream.
Well, it might be said, at this hour
he is half in dream and half in the real world.

Who can predict when, in what direction the person
walking in sleep will make a move,
Whose door would he knock at, whose bolt
rap at,
on the way which characters of what folk tales will
he come across,
what places will he visit that he visited never.
His restless soul will make him wander, nobody
knows where.

What incomplete dreams they are
that searching out he has stepped out on the
road in sleep itself.
What tensions they are that even in his sleep he is not
at peace with himself.

At this hour when it's past midnight and he is on
the road
his head is so near with the moon that sometimes
when his hair waves in the wind it hides the moon
behind it.
On the shoulder of the person walking in the sleep
a cloud is resting the way |
as if a hawk is sitting on it.
He is cut off from the entire skyscape.
No sound as such is reaching his ears.

Suppose if suddenly he wakes up at this moment,
what shall happen.
The pieces of the sun sleeping in his pupils,
will scatter here and there.

Walking in his sleep, he will pass away
right before us.
Wonderstruck we shall see, isn't that he a piece of looking
glass,
isn't that he were we ourselves only
walking in sleep.

11.09.97

Her household

Just returned from her office
tired and lost
keeps the tiffin box in the kitchen
splashes water on the face
ties her loose string of hair back
presses her eyes softly with her palm
gets up and starts to move towards kitchen
I say, "You remain seated, I shall prepare the tea today".
The tip of my voice punches me
Start boiling water after lighting the gas
Just the next moment, I call
Listen where is the sugar
and where are the tea-leaves ?
She enters thrusting
the end of her sari into her waist
She says while pushing me away
"Move, you won't be able to find anything"
Smiles in a different way while twisting her lips
It's very difficult to understand
the exact meaning of that smile
As if she says
It's my creation
You won't be able to understand ever
in which clouds are the rains
and in which the cotton is kept

While opening some boxes, she says
It's me who has managed everything
Otherwise, you won't be able to trace yourself
Go out and watch the TV
You won't do even a single thing
and disturb my entire kitchen.

Itching at the back

Have just returned after finishing all odd jobs,
eating the evening meal,
changing the clothes,
have just pushed myself in bed in the hotel
and off and on it's itching at the back
it's here now that you are coming to the mind off and on.
Of course, 'Janeu', the holy thread could be a great
help at the moment
but that I had left long back
on the peg of the ancestral house.
Moreover, there isn't any bullock cart here
resting against the wheel of which
I might scratch my back.
Stretching over the back,
I reach my hand
to the extent it can
but this irritation in skin annoys me,
every time it slips beyond the reach of my hand.
Beyond the limit of my hand, it's your palm
that I am reminded of.
What a fine excuse your thoughts have jumped
to visit my mind
such a long way from home
in this pink city.

Her countenance

Suddenly blew out the light.
It became pitch dark all around.
She fumbled at the matchsticks
and lighted a candle.

Sectioned between half-light and half-dark
lined up her countenance.
After how long a time, not certain,
I saw her countenance this way
as I saw the earth
from some other planet.

08.04.99

Two small socks

While taking out things from the box of old clothes,
suddenly appeared those two small woollen socks.

Came to the memory those days when sitting in the warm afternoon sun,
glancing intermittently at her stomach, smiling in
heart of hearts, the wife would keep them knitting.

It's of those days when we were expecting
our first daughter.

After such long years, have come up to the sight these socks suddenly
as there rushes to the memory something of childhood.
So small are these socks that in deep astonishment
is steeped my daughter's face,
that sometime so very small were her feet.
Perhaps it's in the very small and simple things only that
there remain so much of intimacy and so much
of tickling.

They are two small socks or a ghosts' strides
that have taken me in the afternoon thirteen years back.

How easily travels such a long distance,
the smell of the two small feet pervading
the two small socks.

Chappals

In the *Drawing Book of Devilal Patidar* these are the chappals
drawn in lamp-black and charcoal.

These haven't returned from nor these have any eagerness
for journeys
nor have these the imprints of sweat of anybody's feet,
nor dust nor mud,
nor any hectic fever nor a sense of waiting,
nor have these on them any price slip, nor
any company's seal.

Any falsehood as such can't put them on for
it has no feet
and truth won't wear them for these aren't chappals at all
but are their shadow.
These are above truth and falsehood,
above the need of the both.

In what space and time these exist,
it's difficult to say.
These might be existing in the midst of some
boundless sky
and can well transcend any space of time.

To whatsoever extent motionless may be a chappal,
there's definitely in it some or other dream of a journey.

04.07.95

What's the name of that plumber

I have read the lives of a great many dictators of
the world,
know a great deal also about many dangerous murderers,
can tell a lot of intimate things about so many
high officials that shot the headlines
in scams and sex scandals.

And can speak fluently for an hour about
the badly rotten politicians
but past an hour trying hard and not
recollecting at this moment the name of that plumber
who had been here a number of times to set right
the oft-repeated problems in our pipeline.
Where does he live, where his meeting point,
don't remember anything
and as for his family
oh! I am such a sorry figure!

It's quite shocking, what a great deal I know about the
bad sorts
and know lots and lots about those who are worse,
while any problem in the pipeline was ever
set right by any dictator, his biography makes
no mention as such.

At this juncture, its only women who come to your help.
It's rather surprising but it's an undeniable truth
that women and women only know most about the

people who rush to help you in critical hours,
who know the art of setting right the little disturbances
of life.

The wife knew that four days back
a new babe was born at the sweeper's,
she, for her newborn was taking out the clothes
of our daughter's childhood that time.
When badly puzzled, I called her out,
listen .... what's the name of that plumber?

04.05.99

Echo

Now she resounds only the last word of your
spoken sentence.

You can't see her or though, you see, you
wink at her.
But from vales desolate, domes filled with sad memories,
caverns and wells dried up long back,
she keeps reverberating
the last letters of your sentence.

You often do speak those words only
that you want to listen to time and again.

It's said once she was a chatterbox,
her tongue worked like a pair of scissors
and she was always short of time for talking endlessly.

Many a time, I feel,
had womenfolk like menfolk spoken little,
how lonesome would have looked this earth
and kids would have taken how long a time as to learn
that how to speak.

She would babble that much
that the rivers as lost in her conversation would
forget to flow,
the winds stopped as to listen to her words,
clouds would pitch their camps on points not designed
for camping.

But they say Hera, one day cursed her and snatched away
all her voices.

That's why as having lost your way in dense forests,
when you called out someone loudly,
she would but repeat your last words,
she couldn't ever reply your any question.

She continued walking along with you like a shadow.
She lost away her dreams and her loquaciousness.
She, that you always winked at, made her presence felt
even in her absence
and kept reverberating the last letters of
your every spoken sentence.

10.10.96

Relating to learning as how to drive a car at an advanced age

It's really a task to learn to drive a car
at an advanced age.
When we return, after putting in some practice, it's not
the body
but the mind
that gets so tired that we become a corpse.
The moment we are on the bed
there's no rest even on the bed,
while lying there, it suddenly occurs to us
that we are driving a car
and a child running throws itself right before the car,
we forget to blare the horn and
as to brake, in consternation, we press our foot
and the accelerator gets pressed by mistake ...
Accident!
A horrible accident all of a sudden,
perspiring to the bone, almost frightened, we open our eyes,
the heart beats like anything.
At an advanced age, it's really a task to learn to
drive a car
as we advance in age, we want to save life,
ours and that of others
At an advanced age, we fear accidents, have forebodings,
the romance is subsided and reason starts asserting far
more

heart comes to the mouth when sitting in a vehicle
exceeding the normal speed.
We want to avoid getting ourselves into any damned new
trade or a risk.
Obstinacy won't do at an advance age,
of course, we boast of doing all that that's the youngster's
territory,
but someone asserts within,
'NO, that you can't do'
just to fight out our shame, we say,
'but now at this age,
it doesn't behove us to do all that'
It's not easy to learn to drive a car

At an advanced age
horrible reveries haunt us all the time.
Time and again we make mistakes, fear changing gears.
The instructor shouts at us time and again, tells
'Sir, you are so senior that it looks odd to shout at you'.

Time and again he gets annoyed and pities us,
time and again he makes us realise our age.

The unfulfilled wish

There always comes out the story of the unfulfilled wish
when turning on talks this or that time.
It's never possible to forget it completely.

It's really difficult to say that there deep within
what the unfulfilled wish builds or demolishes.
Sometimes it's in our dreams that it realizes its fulfilment,
sometimes it pinches like some acute pain, hidden
and without any good reason and at no proper hour,
brusting into a loud laugh we veil over the tears
rising deep inside.

A number of times catching hold of the finger of their
unfulfilled wish, people take themselves to the ways that
it becomes difficult to trace them out again.
With a gesture of pity people will remark,
'What a promising chap he was'. Hadn't he gone astray,he
would have performed a marvel.

It's not a poet, I wished to be a doctor
but circumstances didn't allow the realization of this wish.
By the way, the laws of economics have no respect for
any wish as such.

Such was the trend of our time
that the parents with average income dreamt their son
or daughter to be a doctor.
So typical was our entire medical machinery
that this wish every time, expressed itself irresistibly.

As to fall ill here was such a troublesome and costly affair
that everybody wished a doctor in one's own house
that one's old age may pass comfortably.
Civil hospitals were like the fantasies,
wherein a patient would look for the doctor for whole of
the day
and one day he happened to meet God who would say
to him, 'Come on, it's your time to depart'

The days when my parents were hatching like an egg
of some golden bird their wish to see me a doctor,
I too, sometimes dreamt myself as putting on a white
apron and a stethoscope hung round the neck.
But neither theirs nor my wish saw any fulfilment.
I turned out to be a good-for-nothing fellow and took
to writing poems
and that too, not up to the mark.

That unfulfilled wish of mine always haunts me.
My eyes fall on the diseases spreading hither and thither,
as a teacher's eye every time rests on the spelling errors.
More than often it's a case with me that even unasked
of, I start giving everybody a piece of advice.

Though it's beyond an apothecary
to cure the illnesses of our times.
Not necessary that my prescriptions will definitely serve
anybody.

The unfulfilled wish was like that diary, that was left half way
but that couldn't be ever thrown out.

It was too an unfulfilled wish that would reveal itself
sometimes without,
sometimes in poetry.

The joint family

Before my dropping in, he has turned back.
There in the lock of the house, his slip is stuck.

God knows what made him come over here.
Volumes might he have to speak to me,
has gone back all along with him.
On his way to me, might be, he hasn't drunk a drop
of water, thinking that it's here with me that he would
have his cup of tea.
How does it feel when someone this way turns back from
the house.

No one might have ever turned back this way
from that ancestral house of childhood.
Grandpa, grandma, mother and father were there.
Though quarreled and squabbled, all brothers and sisters
lived together.
There always stayed someone or other in the house.
Every visitor would be given a welcome at least for
a second or two,
would be offered a glass of water and a piece of jaggery
He would collect information of one who was out of the
station.
Rarely anyone might have turned back looking at the lock.
A lot has disintegrated, really a lot, in the process of
disintegration.
Now hardly three people live there in this house.

When going out somewhere, all go out together
leaving the house desolate.

This small single family.
When one is out, to others
the house is ghostly.

The new trend has smoothed the course
of the burglars.

Get-togethers are rare.
People are becoming more and more
strangers to one another,
even in hours of joy and sorrow, people come
not together as they did in former times.
Congrats and condolences reach telegraphically.

Grandpa was known all over the town.
Three four localities took not even father to be a stranger
and as for me even my next door neighbour doesn't know
what name I go by.
Now it's only in the album
that the family people live together.
Nobody ever thinks, what has disintegrated
and what hasn't,
in this process of disintegration.

Someone has turned back from the house,
having looked at the lock.

24.02.93

Nail cutter

This nail cutter is there in our house for years together.
Well, it can be called ancestral.

My grandpa did trim his nails with this very cutter.
He was very punctual and wouldn't get his beard shaved
off on Thursday.
He never stepped out of the house bareheaded.
When someone would walk dragging his feet or playing
the chappals,
he would become rather furious.
He exercised such an awe that during his life
Ma dared not ever to be in the balcony.
He was Nabob's subordinate and wore 'achkan'.

During the Freedom Fight he had never been in the jail
anytime.

This nail cutter is there in our house for years together.
My father, too, always trimmed his nails with this very
one.
He would smoothe round the remaining edges of the
nails
with the file joined to the nail cutter.
Once when Gandhiji passed through the town,
he had been to the station to have a glimpse of him.
They say it created an uproar in the house.
That Khadi kurta and pyajamas bought stealthily,

after that day he never put on even in his bed.
He never spoke to anybody in a baritone.
After sometime he became a storekeeper in the British
cantonment
and after Independence became the headclerk in the
Government Treasury.

This nail cutter is there in our house for years together.
It neither ever got rust nor it ever became blunt.
In my childhood, while at an inspection in the school,
they found my nails uncut.
That day I had a good scolding both at school
and at home.
After that my elder sister would trim my nails regularly.

This nail cutter is there in our house for years together.
Now it's with this nail cutter only that I cut my nails.
Rubbing against the file, smoothe round the edges left over.
I do not remember for how many years, I didn't say 'no'
to anybody.

22.08.97

Hands

Sir, every hand has its own knack.

Talking of this or that tact in this or that hand,
you always happen to meet, someone or other,
somewhere or other,
sometime or other.

Now, you take an example of my maternal grandfather.
They say he had a magic of a cure in his hand.
People from distant villages, overloading bullock carts,
would rush to him for their treatment.
The person who had been once to him, wouldn't peer, even
unheededly into any other doctor's.
It was spoken of him ' If Doctor Sa'b would give you
even chalk ground to dust, the dead would come back to life.
The dacoit Chandan Singh's skull was chopped by his
enemies with a battle-axe and separated like a bowl,
even then Doctor Sa'b kept him alive no less than twelve
hours.

For that matter, no less famous were 'the baflas'[5] as
prepared with granny's hands,
but she had no match in cooking the 'Arhar Dal'.
Measuring out in her fingers, just approximately, she
would put in all spices
but you wouldn't dare say that salt was less or chilli sharp
sometime.

---

5. made of wheat flour or dough, boiled and baked, a delicious dish

Mother and her sisters left no stone unturned
but none's had the taste that granny's hand had.
And the Samosas prepared by the maternal aunt,
middle one,
were stories-like narrated in the whole family.

As many hands as were there in the world, there were as
many arts, as many insights.
Every hand had its own magic, its own marvel,
And Rana, the great, you too, must have heard his name.
He was a great magician of our old small Bhopal.
It's said even Gogiya Pasha saluted the superb
trickery of his hand.

06.03.99

Umbrellas

During the days of rains with showers
slant and broad like the stripes on the back of a leopard
or when sometimes the sun is scorchingly hot,
our umbrellas rush to the memory.
From some corner or the loft of the house, they are taken out.
Removing some old piece of cloth or paper wrapped round
them, their twigs and canopy are critically examined.

When put up straight on our heads they look as
one more patch of sky beneath a broader sky,
in this tortuous time filled with forebodings and tyranny.
Some corner far more safe and intimate,
one more brief span of time, quite personal.
With them often there is associated the memory of some woman.

Very much like the skies of the rains, their cloth
has turned blackish and discoloured
but there in some corner keeps gleaming
the first letter of either our or father's name,
that the younger sister embroidered with silk-threads years ago.
There don't grow dim the tints of those threads.

Countless memories of the rains throng the heart.
Umbrellas do step in them like a character.

With them are there associated the remembrances of
those films also
in which standing under a single umbrella, Raj Kapoor and
Nargis, would soak themselves continuously
in an attempt to protect each other.
Sometimes I think, if there had been an umbrella in
Gandhiji's hand,
would he have looked to us far more Indian.

Sometimes our umbrellas are left behind in some journey
or in market or somewhere else ...
There is left, keep leaving a lot,
with the passing of age
A lot that is deeply personal is left, somewhere without,
whither
no one knows.

27.06.95

The longing for home

Sitting on the broken bench of the wayside hotel,
eating buns dipping in tea, suppress with difficulty
rising in the heart like a call, the longing for home

A sadness pounces upon the face,
caught in the frenzy of the country wine, there comes
staggering
a Master of a Primary School, threadbare, with a thump
sits by my side
and grumbles, 'They have thrown me here in the jungle,
two hundred fifty miles from home.'
These past ten years I have put in hundreds of
applications,
have taken rounds and rounds of the Department of
Education,
frittered away my entire salary on the buses of State
Transport,
drunk the water of countless sheds of hotels, taken in
their salt,
have thrown into my mouth pounds of dust.

Nobody lends me his ears,
no rascal is ready to listen to me.

The greatest tragedy of our times is to be thrown in exile
How, how should I show him my suffering,
putting on a face of someone looking in distance,
I avoid my gaze at him.

Nobody knows, cursing whom and how many,
suddenly the Master breaks into sobs.
People standing around look at, as though
watching a 'tamasha'[6.]

How clownish becomes our sorrow,
the moment it comes out!

There in the distant skies shrieks
some 'tithari'[7]
returning to its nest.

11.05.89

---

6. one of the forms of drama.
7. street-play, a bird.

The Ominous village

That stood by me in my hardest of days,
gave me a job,
arranged my bread and butter,
of that village ask not the name,
it's name is not called out.

The best potato of this province grew here,
carpets of the coarse yarn were woven there
that were called 'doriya'
and it was in great demand far and wide.
There the land was fertile and the wells had water,
in the late hours of night when you saw people speculating on,
you could read out that people had money in their purse
but of that village, ask not the name
It's name is not called out.

After marketing when people would return from the other village,
They would ask of the conductor for the ticket,
nobody would call the name of that village,
in place of its name they would say - eleven miles.
Sometimes someone jokingly would say
'one ticket', the ominous village,
and all of them would burst into a long loud laugh.
This one that would give all at least once
an excuse to laugh
of that village ask not the name,
it's name is not called out.

02.11.98

Preservation

There enclosing with her palms, a woman
is protecting the tremulous flame of the earthen lamp
from being blown out.
A very very old woman humming in a weak voice,
is making listen to her younger daughter-in-law
the song that she herself heard sometime from her own
mother.

There a child is trying to lift up
an ant fallen into water on a green leaf.
There a man pasting the photographs of his kins in an
album,
is telling his son the stories of his grandparents, maternal
and paternal.

The world continues to be
that someone or other, somewhere or other, every moment
is preserving something or other
worth preserving.
Right now some people have traced out those books
that recorded the techniques as to prepare the plaster of the
ancient buildings of this town

Now the old dilapidated buildings standing in the 'Khirni'
ground are being renovated with that finesse of bygone
times.

22.06.99

The streets of our town - one

The streets of our town had so many bends and curves
and were roundabout.
The ways of some streets wended through the skies.

Wandering through those streets, a number of times the
stars
crossed our way like the farmers returning from
the expanse along with their lanterns.
Without any good reason they would start chatting with
us and to some extent would accompany us to show the
way.
Sometimes the moon also would come to our sight
wandering
or sitting at the sill of the sky.
Like the coin of some old State, now thrown out of the
market,
her face would be palled sometimes, sometimes would
glisten
like the bronze platter brightened after scrubbing it hard.
Perhaps like us, she too was either jobless or a vagabond.
Shuffling in the night was in her habit.

These were the days when between our dreams and
reality
there continued an endless quarreling.
We had come from the low-roofed houses, the doors
of which were so small that the moment you raised your

neck, your head would dash against the frame of the
door.
We were in a bad habit of dreaming.
We would cry after a movie and avoided looking directly
in the eyes of reality.

When we had footsore after continuous wandering,
we would sit on the board of the shop with shutters
down
or on a small bridge.
Someone would fumble his pocket and take out a round
of 'bidis' and would light up the 'bidis' for all.
In the light of the stick the entire phantasma would
crack for the fraction of the moment.

Jumping up the sky would go very high
and beneath the feet there jutted out the uneven cobbles
of the streets.
Residing for generations together in this very town, even
the quill-sharp occupants
didn't have the idea that what a number of
bends and curves were there in the streets of this town
and how roundabout they were
that the ways of a great many streets wended through
the skies.

02.05.99

The Streets of our town - two

If we were on foot and in a great hurry to reach
somewhere,
the streets would greatly shorten a number of long ways.
By the way there was such a network of those streets
spreading all over the town
that even without stepping out on the roads, the entire
town could be measured wandering through those streets.
Through those streets, a number of streets would go to
our dreams.

As to gossip on there were pockets with endless leisure, in
those streets,
There were boards projecting out of shops and houses.
When in late night they became desolate,
chess was unrolled on them.
On those squares of light and shade, there kept moving
almost till midnight the pieces black and white.
It's from these boards that there came out that champion
of our State, Rafiq.

They say he was a disciple of Babu Khan
who had a great skill in outmatching that game-trick
they called Shuturghunna.

In the streets there were innumerable small tea-shops,
there in the shops were rooms pushing inside,
wherein one or sometimes two carrom-boards were placed.

In these rooms choked with the cigarette-smoke and the
pale dim light
the players of carrom would keep sitting all the night
over.
There outside on the carrom of the sky, like the last white
piece spared as to cover after the queen, the moon would
be placed.
The roads would often go by the names of dukes and
duchesses
while the streets would go by the names of the people
who had never been recorded in history.

The street of Kali Dhobin, the street of Sheikh Batti, the
street of barbers, the street of the Band Players, the street
of the Gulia Dai....
it's on one end of this street that Jumma Pahlwan lived
who every year would frame the Ten-headed of Dushara,
on the other end there was the house of Khushilal Vaidya
whose one of the sons was elected the President of this
country past these days.
When the moon mounted high on the domes of Jama
Masjid,
the mysteries of the streets would deepen.

Even during the days of hardships, these streets did never
anytime put us to shame.
Amidst the riots, they provided us with the ways to reach
our homes
Thanks to them that the town never looked to us
unfriendly.

05.08.99

Ahad Hotel

I should tell you Ajmal Kamal that
the position of Ahad Hotel was quite distinct
from the other tea-shops of the town.

Whether the notorious gangsters of the town,
the small or the big shots of the political parties
or the litterateurs of Hindi and Urdu,
would always be there glued to different tables.

I should tell you Azmal Kamal
that right in the middle of that market of Ibrahimpura
narrowing into a lane
where there stands now a grand shop of shining shoes,
sometimes flourished that Ahad Hotel.
From the hectic and howling time of the market
was quite different the face of time pervading there inside
the hotel.
Of people taken to be merry idlers it was such a
rendezvous

where sittings and gossipings hours on end could go
with no nudge or poking in.
The thing was that Azmal Kamal that the most jolly poet
of the town Janab Taj Bhopali used to be the manager
of the hotel those days.

I should tell you Azmal Kamal
that the first duchess of the State, Fatah Bibi had no child
as such.

Of course, when she was well advanced in age, she
adopted a boy by name of Ibrahim.
It was that very name that the locality was called by.

In the beginnings the Muslim traders dominated the
market.
Then the aftermath of partition brought the expatriates.
In no time the face of the market began to change.

You never happened to meet Atiq-ur-Rahaman, Azmal
Kamal.
That schoolmate of mine always used to speak a phrase,
'The adopted children, usurped the market named after
the adopted child.'

Azmal kamal!
The lights became far more dazzling every day
and the contours of the market were getting transformed
quickly.
The chatting and the gossip-corners were shrinking.
It looked the tailor there sitting high above the skies
was rather scissoring shorter and shorter the fabric-roll of
our day.
Despite this Ahad Hotel stayed unimpaired in its place
And even then one would get there tea in a big cup full
to the brim to one's heart's desire.

I should tell you Azmal Kamal
that there in the very hall that was on the ground floor in
Ahad hotel
was a balcony not much above one's height, wherein were
fitted
the carved glasses of Belguim,
there Mazhar Pathan and his chums would make their den
day in, day out.

Sometimes, in the lower hall, when no table was in spare,
even then nobody would dare to go to the balcony for
tea.
Quite close to the door there was a counter behind which
Taj Saheb would sit on a tall stool.
Sometimes when Muktibodh and Parsaiji visited the town,
people say, it's here with Mathura Babu that they had their
long sittings.
By and by people who stood witnesses to these stories
and discourses are vanishing away.
Leaving the counter, Taj Saheb too, would have his
rounds
intermittently of those tables
where seated the litterateurs of that era.
Aftab used to say
that between the two lines, sometimes is heard
the sound of Taj Saheb's approaching footfalls thief-like.

I should tell you Azmal kamal
that in those days that Ahad hotel had begun to prick
like a-thorn in the eye of the market.
With great detestation, the shopkeepers around would
remark
'these idlers and good-for-nothing sorts have clutched up
such a big chunk of market in the centre.'
People as such didn't have a very good opinion of those
who hauntred the hotel all the day long.
Since the bulk of the frequenters was that of the writers
and the members of the Communist party, it was in
the air that all the people sitting there, were communists.

In those days they used to speak about the inspector
who just took charge of the Police Station, City
that he was a son of a bitch.

Standing before the hotel he swore
that 'one day I would bring this hotel to dogs'.

Azmal kamal what should I tell you,
whether the inspector was in luck or ours was a bad lot,
it's in those very days that a thing did happen there in
the hotel,
that was the first or you might say the last incident at that
hotel.
The news of the hostile clash and stabbing between
Mazhar Pathan and Shafiq Pathan spread like a wild fire
and that's how the police inspector of the City Police Station
kept his vow to bring Ahad hotel to ruinage.

That's how one day Ahad hotel
pricking like a thorn in the eye of the police
and the traders, met its doom.
Gradually there came to an end the dens of discourses
between the writers and intelligentia.
With the bedimmed memories of Ahad Hotel.
dimmer and dimmer became all the bonds between
the people.

Azmal Kamal,
that's what one complete fresco of our times
and one delightful burlesque too,
that the space that was once studded with beautiful
words,
now is stuffed with shining shoes
and they are laden neither with dust of a journey
nor with the smell of some foot's sweat.

08.09.99

Three Elegies

(in memory of Nirbhik Verma 'Kappu')

Elegy - one

So brief a life and this number of tribulations.

You died going there in a town not yours
and in your own town, like a piece of trifle news
has reached your demise.

For your untimely death,
the ill-turns of your habits are being explored.
Perhaps this is the only way the friends resort to
as to enable them to bear the sorrow.
The habits that will be taken to be cause of your death,
tales related only with them will be told
every time with a sauce,
that's how they all will little put off their grief.

How isolated we have been made by our times and society.
Even the dear ones aren't exception to it.
But let us think over it some other time.
Who would like to be in a great agony,
who likes to have a peep within.

I can't face your death,
that it's along with you that has died
the one in me
that could ever encounter
such an hour.

Elegy - two

From everything associated with our childhood we were
thrown apart,
we were rooted out from our streets, boards and soirees.
It has been snatched away from us
just for trivial needs.

Suppose we talk it to someone, he will say
you are foolishly growing sentimental.
There's nothing unlikely in it,
as for the custom to be in love with the places,
it has died long back.

We didn't dream big things,
had no cravings at all.
We never regretted our hardships.
Despite our barest needs we could not be
allowed to stay in this big town.

We couldn't ever throw out from us
wherefrom we were thrown out.
We couldn't ever have a root
wherein we were planted.

Our sorrow was that nature
that it wasn't possible to name it sorrow.
Who will after all take it to be
a cause of our death.

Elegy - three

Talking to friends my throat is getting choked time and again
and there flashes on the memory that afternoon
when you suddenly broke into tears
and sat down there on the pavement of New Market.
As to grow sentimental this way wasn't the nature of our
relations.

A garb of recklessness we had put on,
ours was a stubborness not to speak our sorrow to
anybody.
We always posed to be damned careless.

Nobody there stood a witness to our exile and
breathlessness
nor was there any to share our sorrows.
We ourselves, too, were
not so much involved in each others suffering.

Our postures as such
made no room for our weeping.

I spare the eyes that they get wet
and with a cough inside repeatedly clearing
my throat of lump
and you.

You have quitted past
all the troubles of facing life.

Now the curtain falls

(in memory of the young dramatist, Sanjeev Dixit)

Now the curtain falls.

In the wedlock of life rather soaked in blood,
dodging the murderers bearing the battle-axes,
he has fallen in the hands of Death's witch.

Now nothing can be done.
His stage-back is impossible in the next scene.
We have by ourselves to deliver the dialogues to come,
he won't be giving us any clue,
His part will be left blank in the following scene.

The witch of death has taken him away,
hiding him in her green shawl.
The moon will rise and look for him around,
lending her ears will have a hint of his footfalls,
from nowhere will there swim in his voice,
nowhere will there haunt his shadow.

In frozen frescoes have been arrested all his movements.
Resounding the entire jungle with their hooves, the horses
are passing.
Running with senses all alert, looking all around
he is not there.

In his absence, it is not possible now to drag the scene on.
Sitting in the midst of the audience, a small child asks,

when Papa shall appear,
with the border of her garment, a woman is hiding her
tears.

A friend of mine has left not to come back.
Now the curtain falls.

21.10.93

The girl's age there in the photograph

When that boy had his admission
in Post-graduation in the Drawing School,
the same year came to the School
a girl by name of Magee Fernandes.
She was older than boy by two years.
Going to the office of the school he had seen
the girl's date of birth in the Application Form.

Every Sunday Magee would go to the Woodhouse
Church for her prayers.
The boy though a non-believer, also started going for
prayers.
Standing by the side of the girl, he would inhale the
fragrance of her hair.
Magee's father was some official in the Railways
and Magee lived in the upper storey of a house in the
Churchgate Railway colony.
There were a great many dogs in the colony and they
barked terribly.
Though it's not of much relevance here
but it's something of the times of the World War II.
The horrible news regarding Hilter kept pouring in.
The boy had no such fright of Hitler
as he had of the dogs of the colony,
that were in packs and packs and barked like anything.

War being the reason, most of the houses were left
desolate.

It's from there that the boy watched Magee coming and
going, entering the bath and taking off her clothes.

It's a story of one night
when Magee, turning off the lights, had slipped in her bed,
the boy passed by her house.

There a policeman pounced upon him
taking him to be a vagabond.
For whole of the night, the boy kept lying in the lock-up,
the mosquitoes and the bugs stung him all the night long.
On Magee's father's evidence that the boy had been there
to meet the girl,
the boy was released next day.
Of course, in the meantime, the bugs and the mosquitoes
bred up in that damp cell of the police station had
sucked up pretty lot of his blood.
The cell was far worse than the jails that the boy had read
about
in the novels of Alexandre Dumas.

The boy was just barely seventeen.
Hence misfortunes couldn't swerve him.
But this adventure bore one sweet fruit.
What the boy couldn't speak to Magee even these so
many days,
Magee came to know.
And Magee became rather cautious about the windows
around.
After some days she too started having fun in this game.
Now when she would have a look at herself in the mirror,
would also look at the windows of the houses around as

mirrored in the glass, with the corners of her eyes and
when

she would intuit that the boy was gazing through some window,
a number of times she would let rustle down the garment from her shoulder the way
as if she didn't know that someone was watching her.
Something of narcissism was in it and self-display too.
Love hasn't sprouted as yet.
The boy one day suddenly fell ill
and he had to move to his father's house, some other town.

Then passed a number of days,
a number of months passed then,
then passed years and years.

After years together the boy once again came to the same town.
The girl had been married off.
She had gone to Dubai along with her husband.
She had two children also.
One day the boy called on Magee's father,
Magee's mother showed the boy one of Magee's photographs.
There in the photograph Magee still stood the same age that the boy had loved her.

Time couldn't wither the beauty of the girl
there sitting in the photograph.

10.11.98

His victory

Fifteen years back, on one warm morning of April third,
he killed himself.

Of all his was the smallest size
but he was the most conspicuous amongst all.
Every time he won over, I kept losing to him all the time.

When his legs could hardly reach the pedals,
he learnt that how to ride a bicycle.
He would win over the marbles of all boys and making
them sound kept roaming in the whole school.
Till some girl dawned on us,
he would go and make friends with her.
As to play truants, we would look for the moment,
that the Master Sa'b turned his back,
he would have already stepped out,
and before we stepped out, he would have been there in
the cinema hall.

Of all he was the first to start smoking and drinking too.
In matters of women, he was the most experienced.
He speculated surpassing all.
He always staked high.
He bade the world adieu earliest of all.

He was my age.
Today, when I look in the mirror at my grey hair

and the growing patches of dark under the eyes,
and think
how he would have looked had he survived by this time,
but no imagination as such works,
every time flashes the same face before the eyes
that used to be fifteen years back.
He defies Time. He comes out victorious again.

06.04.98

The shriek of the dream of time

Underneath the moon, from the trunk of a tree
standing in its shadow
there's tied a boat.

The fishermen have already left for their homes.
The wreaths of smoke are rising from the cottages
palm-roofed in the distance.
There's only the rising and falling sounds of the waves.
Behind the boat there's standing a girl, all alone.
She is waiting for someone.

Watching the waves, the girl is thinking,
right now there will emerge a horse rider from
the waves, breaking
from the manes of the horse there will be scattered
the pearls of water.
But from the darkness deepening on the back of the
girl there are coming out
some terrible horsemen in lunch of the girl's dreams.
There's rushing ahead a wild wave of the sea
and the grain of sand beneath the girl's feet are getting
eroded,
the feet of the girl are sinking down.

There swims in a voice from far
'more than oft warned thee not to rush to the
seashore at night'

Thereafter the whole landscape has drowned in dark,
a shriek is all
that goes cleaving the wind to a great far.
It's not that of the girl
but a shriek of the dream of our time
drowning in darkness.

02.05.94

Waiting in the restaurant

Whom she is over here to meet, hasn't turned up till yet.
She repeatedly opens and shuts her purse.
Glances at her watch and assures herself
whether it's keeping time.
An invisible wall is rising round her.
In this unseen round of boredom and anxiety
she is all alone,
as alone as she can be.
The waiter is standing beyond this wall.

The waiter has already placed before her a glass of water.
Rather slowly takes two gulps of water,
and touches the cool glass upon her sore eyes.
She peers beyond the trees
standing outside the restaurant,
as if the trees were transparent.
Standing beyond the unseen wall, the waiter is in a fix,
whether he should move to take orders or not.

Nobody knows from what fever and commotion of life,
she had stolen away this hour
that's slipping like sands slowly and slowly,
She has moved round her chair,
and has sat down turning her back to the door
as if towards hope.

She hears somewhere within herself so quiet
a sound of something cracking.

The sight and the image

There in the open space before a cinema house,
a shining car of a new model
is frightening a crippled child.

The car is gliding on slowly
and the frightened, perplexed staggering child
is desperately trying to run on its heels.

The driver is breaking into a smile
and the onlookers around are getting shivers within.
They pity
but are laughing.

This is one sight
that's changing into an image of our times.

06.11.97

The defeated laugh

The tyrants come over and conquer.

The weak bow down and accept their defeat
Those falling on the battlefield turn into legends
and killing legends is not that easy
as killing man.
The weak ones who survive, by dint of their art and
dexterity, gradually win over the hearts of their masters.
One morning they become the weakness of the masters.
One morning the masters can't do without them.

There comes a morning when the masters' gestures
are those of the slaves.
One morning the masters' faces come to have
the semblance of the slaves.

One morning, the tyrants' brutality looks ridiculous
One morning their wrath looks so miserable.
One morning when they shout at,
the slaves break into a smile.

One morning the tyrants hide their deplorable state
in the mask of a defeated laugh.

23.08.97

Hitler's drawing

That's the story of those days in nineteen hundred eight,
when Hitler did a drawing
of a quiet village with his pencil.
That's the story of those days in nineteen hundred eight,
when the Art Gallery of Vienna second time
disqualified Hitler
for drawing

That small drawing of Hitler had Hitler's signature on it,
hence a magnate of England,
when auctioned this drawing, the size of a postcard only,
and done in pencil,
it sold off for no less than seven thousand British pounds

Was it a price of that so simple a piece of drawing,
was it a price of Hitler's signature,
that he put in one of the corners of the drawing.
Was it created by that brutal war
that spared no such village as was there
in the drawing
or the village that might have been, before that drawing

Hitler, throughout his life
proved right
the judgement of Vienna's Art Gallery.

17.11.98

Shadow

There's a shadow of the stairs on the wall,
on the stair's shadow, the shadows of some men
are climbing up.
Through the shadow of a door,
the shadows that climbed up the stairs
are entering.

On the shadow of the mosquito-screen,
there's lying a shadow of one more man.
One of the shadows that entered through the door,
is taking out a knife from the pocket.
There in the hand of the shadow cast on the wall,
the shadow of the knife is shaking.

On the wall, there's a shadow of a clock
The time as such it is,
is time's shadow
that's passing through the shadow of a clock.

There in the shadow of this scene of murder,
the shadow of blood is falling.

There's isn't any shadow of shriek.

11.09.98

Until I draft an appeal

Until I draft an appeal,
the city is in flames.
Until I rightly spell the appeal
the van announcing curfew is on the move.
Until the appeal is in the press,
the shops are burnt to ashes,
people are killed.

Until the appeal comes out of press,
the appeal is of no use.

Dec., 92

The barbarians were simply barbarians

The barbarians were simply barbarians.
As for their barbarity, they had no logic.
The barbarians were simply barbarians.
They had no banner of any religion as such.
The barbarians were simply barbarians.
They had no trickery of language
nor had they words like regret or repentance.
We have left them ages and ages behind.
The barbarians were simply barbarians.

Dec., 92

Meeting a Satan

There in the tea-shop, he was sitting alone, on a chair in
the corner.
Having a smoke, Satan was very sad.
The tea-cup was there placed before him
and steam was rising from it.
For a man well acquainted with the stories of Iblis,
it was quite surprising to come across some Satan
the way I came across him.

He said "I'm terribly lonely and badly tired too.
Don't you feel that I have become ridiculous and quite
miserable.
Not even a child will get a fright of my horrible acts.
My position now is no more than a toy or a joker.
This world has left my dark deeds far behind.

Sometimes when I take a review of my foregone deeds,
I laugh at myself.
Those deeds of bygone times look pretty childish.
Sometimes I wonder about myself.
Was it myself
that even gods would ask of mercy.

I feel even gods might have been very very backward like me."

Just getting up, he said,
"now you see it yourself,
had it been the earlier times, well, any one would have liked
to drink tea with me this way."

17.04.96

Generally it doesn't happen so

There the snake has caught the kite in its coils,
the lion is bearing hare's planquin.
Generally it doesn't happen so, but is happening

The hollow-mouths laugh at those having a fine set of teeth.
Those with eyes to see, have been charmed by the
blind's charisma.
It's our times paradox.
One who is losing, says he is in gains,
is gaining.

It's totally wrong to think that only the victorious one
is the best one.
Civilizations have been often conquered by the
barbarians.
Anti-clockwise are moving the clock's hands.
The end of the century is bearing the burden of some
past centuries.

Generally it doesn't happen so but is happening.
Drowned in the maddening joy of victory, the great
band of drum-beaters is singing.
There approaches the end of the century, putting an end
to everything.
The mouse is at fists with the tiger.
Generally it doesn't happen so, but is happening.

The nation is becoming destitute of its whole being.

05.07.95

The dilemma of a good poet

How shall a good poet put up with it
that some other poet writes
a good poem.

He will spin his head off, will scratch out his locks.
The good poet will burst into tears
if a number of good poems are written down
around him.

Endless, eternal, imperishable is envy.

No hope, no hopes now in this life.
Alas! his perseverance has proved futile.
With what a great hope he was born
in the world of poetry
but all in vain.
The world is crowded with poets

The great poet will compose himself with great efforts,
will invoke his Muse, his Minerva,
scrupulously cavit at, will drive to dogs
that every good poem which hasn't flowed from his pen.

He won't be at peace with himself,
will smoke away a dozen of cigarettes, and gulp black tea.
What do you take him to be.?
Rarely he will call a poem 'good'
and if mistakenly comes out 'wonderful',
he will have grippings in the stomach.

He will be evasive, won't make any remark
on his contemporaries,
will be talking the foreign poets
all the time.

No one will get to the dilemma
of a good poet.

March, 1985

About some other country and some other time

Not my own, some other country I am talking about
and about some other time
that's not mine.

Though it's a strange coincidence that I was born
in the same country.
It's there that I had my complete education and it's there
that I put myself in many jobs.
My grandparents and great grandfather were cremated
there only and there in the rivers their ashes were
dispersed.
In my life I never visited any other country save this one
but it was rather surprising that its looks resembled
not at all with the country wherein my childhood was
spent
and about which lessons were taught in the schoolbooks,
about which we sang the songs,
in the streets of which we loved and dreamt the dreams
as to spend the whole of life.

Believe me, the country and the time
I am talking about
strike no semblance with its face.

Of course, the time and the country
I am talking about

gave the complete freedom as to argue
provided it dwelt not on the ruler and if it did so
then it ought have favoured him and if against
then the room should have been properly closed and
completely empty.
'Walls have ears' they said.
Even then there was the complete freedom to speak
your whole heart to the walls
and it was a great privilege.
As to be happy and safe, the easiest way was that
better you should have changed yourself in a blossoming
tree nodding its head the way the wind blew.

Once again I would like to tell you that the story that I am
relating is about the country and time
that were not mine
but it was a strange coincidence that I was the native
of the same country
and was bound to live in the same time.

01.09.99

Why did she weep after such long years

Now the whole village came to call her 'Mad Kisni'.
Madness, so deeply they attached with her name
that it looked a natural part of it.

She was Kisna's woman,
so they already called her Kisni.
It was customary in the village
that they called the wives by the first or second names
of their husbands, that they would disfigure.
They called Doctors wife 'Doctorni' and Collector's
'Collectorni'.
What was Mad Kisni's real name, now nobody knew in
the village,
and Kisni, she neither had the sense of her name nor of
her body.

The village was surrounded by the hills of the
Vindhyachal
On one of the hills there stood a fort
and it was the fort that Mad Kisni was at war with.
The fort was visible from every street of the village.
Whenever Mad Kisni's eyes lifted up at the fort,
raising up her mouth she would start firing abuses
and spitting vehemently at it.
Spit sprinkled on her face, sometimes
she would wipe out with the border of her garment,

sometimes would be rather unconscious of it.
When the sun passed through it, it became kaliedoscopic.

****

As there was a fort,
Maharaj Vikram Singh dwelt in it
and he was childless.
Of course, when well advanced in age,
he adopted a son
whom he sent to a distant town
for higher education.
As Vikram Singh was a king, he had king's hobby
for hunting
and there were plenty of tigers in the jungles of the State.
People talked in a hushed up voice,
'because he can't produce a child,
he is there wandering in this and that jungle,
by hunting out poses of his manliness.'
Truth might be whatsoever,
Vikram Singh had killed no less than ninety-nine tigers.
Many tigers he had stuffed with straw.
The stuffed ones so blazed with life
that their very sight would make one's flesh creep,
though the flame had burnt out in their eyes.
Some heads of the tigers would hang from the walls,
skins of some would serve as a carpet in the drawing hall.
They say, it was Maharaj's heartfelt desire to reach
a number of hundred.
Had he reached it he would have earned any title
whatsoever as one hunting the largest number of tigers.

Since there was the dead dearth of jobs in the State,
the job of tale-bearing was in full flourish.

Hoping a child, Maharaj did what not odds.
He married no less than half a dozen times,
took herbs and drugs, this and that
charms did he put on and amulets too, solicited blessings,
fasted, burnt sacrificial fires
but stars didn't favour him and he had no child.
By the way States and the powers of States were a thing
of history.
Since people had tongues in their mouths, they talked
and they talked most about Maharaj, in the village.
Some believed that Mad Kisni's misgivings scourged the
king.
Some said it was the tigress' curse.
One day when Vikram Singh returned from his hunting
expedition, he had two newly-born cubs of a tigress
picked up on the way.

One of them hardly survived a night
and collapsed in the approaching dawn,
but to the other one, Maharaj would keep in chains with
him.

That's how he looked different from those taming the
dogs.
People would smile up their sleeves
and pitied the fate of the cub.

****

There were days that some passion would seize Kisni
right from the morning.
Some day some naughty chap would play on her
quite in the morn,
then for whole of the day Mad Kisni hurled badest
abuses at the fort,

would drive to dogs this and that,
this and that would call hell,
nearing sundown, Mad Kisni, often would fall silent,
as silent as she could be.
For hours together she would be sitting every evening
on the boundary wall of the reservoir built on
the lonely way of the big Mahadeo,
would be mumbling to herself unintelligibly,
would be in a dialogue with a phantom.
As to pry into the sorrows of the people gone off their heads,
we had no technique as such.
Mad Kisni's man worked there at the fort.
Vikram Singh would drink water only from the reservoir
at the temple of Mahadeo built on the other hill,
no less than a mile away.

It was Kisna's duty to fetch water walking the distance
of the two hills.
Putting pitchers filled with water in his carrier, every
day Kisna would take four rounds from the temple
to the fort.

Whether tales are woven in lifetime or not.
There are endless stories after death.
Till one is rounded off,
another is sprouting.

Since the story was in the air, they said
that one day Kisna was caught stealing in the fort
and the next day in the early dawn, he turned round
his eyes.
Those who had a clue kept mum
and those who were blind to everything babbled like
eye witnesses.

When Kisna was brought home they said,
his body had blues all over it.
Along with it there ran one more story
and it was related in whispers and with a great relish
and as many times as it was related
it came to have a certain newness,
adding salt to it was *in gratis.*

It was said that there in the great bath of the fort,
the queens bathed stark naked
and there sitting in the secret-window, Maharaj
would gaze at the bathing queens.
There were the full-sized gorgeous mirrors on the
walls of the great bath
that would reflect the contours of the queen's bodies
from different angles.

It's there that Kisna was caught stealing a look
through a slit of some door of the bath.
If they had put on an open allegation, what a bad
name it would have brought to the queens
Hence they levelled a charge of theft against Kisna
and killed the poor man.

Since it was so, something or other definitely might have
been in it.
Well, truth might be whatsoever,
but that day they tried desperately to make Kisni weep.
Even they bared before her the face of the corpse but not a
single tear trickled in her eye.
She just kept staring at it calmly.

There were so many stories and the ways to relate them
were that many that truth and lie played seek and hide.

How far lies shadowed the truth and truth illumined
itself in lies, couldn't be discerned.
Since they were the fort matters, hence were so
enveloped,
that when took wings, they would travel beyond
proportions.
The sole delight of the secret things was
that they appeared more truthful than truth and
more false than falsehood.

Two

When Maharaj Vikram Singh breathed his last,
his adopted son was quite green
and was having his education in a distant town.
People from ten villages around attended Maharaj's
funeral
but no sooner the funeral procession, descending
from the vale of the fort, entered the village
than a big scene was created there.

Firing abuses vehemently Mad Kisni
time and again, would push herself before Maharaj's bier.
The police repeatedly pushed her away
and she repeatedly pushed herself in the crowd.
The era of feudal states had passed away
and the police of the Republic were Government
employees,
and for them Princes were people who availed privy
purses and privileges.
One more thing. People who knew Mad Kisni were no
less in number than those who knew Maharaj.
Whensoever Mad Kisni would thrust herself in the
crowd,

people taking sides, would make a passage for her
People were enjoying this scene.
It takes no time that hatred against the ruler changes
into a joke.

That was simply a travesty of sorrow and such a grand
travesty that if any heart somewhere ever heaved a sigh
in earnest,
it would have been drowned in the uproar.

Three

For hours on end Maharaj's demise was kept secret.
Nobody was allowed to go in or come out of the fort
during that whole occurrence.
The story goes this far that the physicians and the
homeopaths, kinsmen and attendants
all who were round the Maharaj in that hour
were locked up in a chamber of the fort itself by the
Diwan.
They manoeuvered meticulously that the news
shouldn't be leaked even to the adopted son.
By the way the boy was still a minor.

Maharaj's mother, of course, was alive but became a
decrepit
that she had nothing to do with the goings on in the fort.
There in one of the corners, she was sitting quiet and sad.
She would put off her spects intermittently and wipe out
the lids of her eyes with the border of her garment.
The cub of the tigress had now come of age.
From some cell, its grunt could be heard
with timely breaks.

****

There in the conspiracies and intrigues of the fort
wasn't anything that looked unnatural.
If there was a miracle then it was only one miracle
that day in the village
that when nobody smelt it in the whole village
before the official announcement,
Mad Kisni had rather got it mysteriously
that Maharaj had passed away.

Right from the morn, Mad Kisni kept howling in
whole of the village..., 'dead, the rogue is dead,
posed to be Maharaj, scoundrel...'
She was volleying out turbulently all the abuses she
had in her stock.
Time and again her throat got choked
and coughing shattered her
but the violent flow of bad language knew no pause.
Of course, people reprimanded her too, twice or thrice,
but Mad Kisni was a fury that day.

People were astonished when the news of Maharaj's
demise reached the village.
It amazed them how Mad Kisni sensed Maharaj's death.
Between the oppressor and the oppressed, what
strange relationship was it|
that Mad Kisni would intuit well in advance each
fair or foul doing in the fort.
'What's going on, in which pocket of the fort
and at what time, Mad Kisni could presage,
unerringly at any moment.

    ****

When the cremation fire was put in Maharaj's pyre.
There abruptly fell a silence all over the crematorium.

Those who were to make a salutation fire, turned
rather into statues.
Sitting beside the pyre, Mad Kisni was wailing her heart
out.
Her wailings would make the wind tremble.

Why did Mad Kisni wail, no one could have an insight.
What rock of abhorrence was it
that had cracked suddenly.
No one could fathom the depth of Mad Kisni's heart.

What lamentation was it, one couldn't say
that had burst out after such long years.

20.04.99